ZONDERKIDZ

The Berenstain Bears®: Jobs Around Town

Requests for information should be addressed to:

Zonderkidz, *Grand Rapids, Michigan 49530*

Library of Congress Cataloging-in-Publication Data

Berenstain, Stan, 1923–2005.
[Berenstain Bears on the job]
The Berenstain Bears : jobs around town / by Stan and Jan Berenstain with Mike Berenstain.
p. cm.
Summary: Brother and Sister Bear speculate on all the things they could grow up to be, including a bus driver, farmer, scientist, singer, and computer programmer.
ISBN 978-0-310-72286-1 (softcover)
[1. Occupations—Fiction. 2. Bears—Fiction.] I. Berenstain, Jan, 1923–. II. Berenstain, Mike, 1951– III. Title: Jobs around town.
PZ7.B4483Berky 2011
[E]—dc22 2010026716

Editor: Mary Hassinger
Art direction: Cindy Davis

Printed in China

---

10 11 12 13 14 15 16 17 /LPC/ 13 12 11 10 9 8 7 6 5 4 3

“In the same way, let your light
shine in front of others.
Then they will see the good
that you do.”

—Matthew 5:16

Previously published by Random House as
The Berenstain Bears On the Job, 1987

The Berenstain Bears®
Jobs Around Town
by Stan and Jan Berenstain
with Mike Berenstain
ZONDERVAN.com/
AUTHORTRACKER
follow your favorite authors
Living Lights™
ZONDERkidz

In Bear Country, there are many jobs to be done. Mama takes care of our tree house and family. Papa does chores and makes fine furniture to sell. But there are other jobs too. And if you pick the right job, work will be fun.

Let's take a trip around Bear Country and see what we might be when we grow up.

HONEY STO

Some jobs can be
exciting. We could fight
fires like Firebear Bob.

Or we could be policebears like Officer Marguerite. She tells us when to safely cross the road. If we don't obey, she blows her whistle …

We might be Beartown bus drivers. Or we might learn to drive a delivery truck, an ambulance, or even a cement mixer.

BEAR COUNTRY
AMBULANCE
AMBULANC
TRUCK CO.

Mama and Papa say God gives everyone a special talent. We can use our talent to do the job that is best for us and help others too.

Some folks are good at fixing things. They might be plumbers, mechanics, carpenters, or watchmakers. Almost everything we use sometimes has to have a fixer!

It would be fun to be a teacher and teach cubs how to read and write…

or a doctor and help make folks well.

We could have a store and sell good things like honey and bread.

Or we could work in a bank where money is kept safe and sound.

Engineers figure out better ways to build things. We could be engineers and build big bridges here in Bear Country.

Scientists study nature and try to find out about new things. Maybe we can become scientists and cure diseases!

We could use our God-given talents to build buildings proud and tall.

Or we might be wreckers and tear down old unsafe buildings. That would be cool—POW!

Brother, do you think my God-given talent is to be a singer? I've always loved to sing!

On second thought, I don't think I should. Maybe I don't really have a singing voice.

Don't worry, Sister, our job hunt is not over yet.

There are so many things to do and be. And the choice is up to you.

You could be an
anchorbear on TV...

and give the news.

You could count the stars
and become an astronomer...

or an astronaut and
visit distant planets
like Jupiter and Mars!

Hey, Sister! Look here. I love computer games. I could work with computers.

But I love Bear Country too. Being an environmentalist and helping stop pollution could be great.

You could be a beekeeper and work with beehives and honey. Mmmmm.

Say, I could be a carpenter like Papa Bear!

Forest rangers protect the trees by watching out for forest fires.

Or we could become farmers like our good neighbor, Farmer Ben.

Mr. and Mrs. Ben raise champion pigs. We could do that on our farm too. Our champion pig would be very, VERY big!

1ST
PRIZE

As farmers, we could use God's good land to grow lots of food for all of Bear Country.

And, oh yes—a word of warning for future farmers: always watch out for the bull!

There are many things to do and be. It can be hard to choose. So if you haven't found the right thing for you …

there's no need to worry. The job for you just may not have been invented yet!

So remember, there are many different kinds of work to choose from. And with God's help, you will pick the right job, help others everyday, and have fun too!